Harry the Clever Spider

Written by Julia Jarman

Illustrated by Charlie Fowkes

Collins

Clare first saw the spider on Saturday.

It was in the bath, trying to climb up the side.

Up and up it went ... then down.

Up and up and up ... then down again.

Again and again, it got half way up, but then –
SPLOSH!

SPLOSH!

"Poor spider, I'll help you," said Clare.
She held out her hand and the spider ran
up her arm, and down again,
and up again.
It tickled and made Clare laugh.

Then the spider did bungee jumps.

Down … and UP.

Down … and UP.

"Wow," said Clare. "I'll take you to school
on Monday. We're doing minibeasts."

4

She saw her brother.

"Charlie, come and look at my spider."

Charlie took one look – and ran!
He jumped onto his bed.
"Take that big, horrible, *hairy* spider away
NOW!" he yelled.

6

Clare laughed. "He's not big and horrible.
Well, he's not horrible."
He was big – for a spider – and he did have
hairy legs.
"I think I'll call him Harry," she said,
as Mum came in.

"Have you two seen my car keys?" said Mum.
Then she saw Harry.
"P-p-please, Clare, take that horrible, hairy
spider away."

Dad saw Harry too.
He said, "Put that hairy monster outside, Clare,
and help us look for the car keys.
Mum's got toothache. We've got to go to
the dentist."

Clare went downstairs but she didn't put
Harry outside.
She put him in a box with a lid on it.
"Spiders like dark places," she said.
"You'll be safer here. On Monday I'll take you
to school."

Clare started to look for the car keys.

Poor Mum.

Toothache was horrible.

She had to get to the dentist quickly.

Clare looked on all the shelves in
the sitting room.
(She didn't see the lid falling off Harry's box.)

She looked on the mantelpiece.
(She didn't see Harry's box fall off the sofa.)

She looked under all the cushions.

(She didn't see what Harry was doing.)

Then Mum and Dad came in.
They saw what Harry was doing.
"Clare!" they yelled. "We said put that spider outside!"

Then Charlie came in.

He saw Harry – and ran out again!

"Mum and Dad told you to put that horrible, hairy monster outside!" he yelled.

But Clare was watching Harry.

Down he went – then up.

Down behind the sofa – then up again.

He was like a yo-yo.

Dad said, "I'll put that spider outside."
But Clare said, "No, Dad. Look at Harry.
He may be trying to help us."

17

Harry went down behind the sofa,
then disappeared.

So Clare looked behind the sofa and ...

... there were the car keys!

"Thank you, Harry," cried Mum.

"Let's go!" said Dad.

"Can I keep him now?" begged Clare.

"Yes!" yelled Mum and Dad.

Only Charlie wasn't happy.

Harry ran up Clare's arm and down again.
She laughed. "You're a big, hairy, helpful spider
... and a very clever one, too!"

Harry can help!

Have you <u>lost</u> something?

Call Harry on : 88881 43567
or email Harry at harryspider@web.net

No Job too small!

What Harry can do

Harry can escape from boxes.

Harry can jump up and down.

Harry can find things.

Ideas for reading

Written by Kelley Taylor
Educational Consultant

Learning objectives: becoming aware of character and dialogue; predicting words from preceding words in sentences; recognising the critical features of words; blending to read words containing consonant clusters in initial position and final position; acting out own and well-known stories, using different voices for characters.

Curriculum links: Citizenship: Animals and us; Science: Plants and animals in the local environment

Interest words: laugh, bungee jumps, toothache, dentist, mantelpiece

Word count: 479

Resources: pencil, black card, silver glitter, PVA glue, black wool, pipe-cleaners, rubber bands

Getting started

This story could be read over two sessions.

- Start by hiding the word 'clever' on the cover and ask the children to use their knowledge of spiders to guess the missing word. Reveal 'clever', and ask children how a spider can be clever.

- Ask them how they feel about spiders. *Why are some people scared of spiders? How might the story's characters feel about Harry?*

- Skim through the book to p21, looking at the pictures, and discuss the different characters – what do they find out about Charlie and Clare?

Reading and responding

- Ask the children to read silently and independently up to p21, intervening when necessary. Ask them to read aloud individually and observe, prompt and praise them when they read with expression and characterisation.

- Remind them to blend sounds together in tricky words, to think 'what would make sense there?' and to use their knowledge of familiar words when reading new words, e.g. *toothache, mantelpiece.*

how2become

A Magistrate

Orders: Please contact How2become Ltd, Suite 2, 50 Churchill Square Business Centre, Kings Hill, Kent ME19 4YU.

Telephone: (44) 0845 643 1299 - Lines are open Monday to Friday 9am until 5pm. Fax: (44) 01732 525965. You can also order via the e mail address info@how2become.co.uk.

ISBN: 978-1-907558-07-8

First published 2010

Copyright © 2010 how2become Ltd.

Typeset for How2become Ltd by Good Golly Design, Canada, goodgolly.ca

Printed in Great Britain for How2become Ltd by Bell & Bain Ltd, 303 Burnfield Road, Thornliebank, Glasgow G46 7UQ.

CONTENTS

CHAPTER I
WELCOME, INTRODUCTION AND PURPOSES

Welcome to your 'insider's' guide to becoming a magistrate.

This guide has been written by people who have worked for many years in the magistrates' courts and who are used to the way in which new magistrates are selected and trained.

The role of a magistrate is clearly one that requires a high level of professionalism and responsibility. As a result of this, there comes a selection process that requires a similar level of preparation. If you want to become a magistrate then you will need to work hard and prepare fully for each stage. Throughout the selection process the assessors will be looking to see whether or not you have the qualities, skills and life experiences to become a competent magistrate. This guide will focus on how best you can demonstrate the required skills at every stage of the selection process.

The 'office' of magistrate (or justice of the peace (JP): terms which are broadly interchangeable) dates back, in one form

or another, to at least 1361. The term 'lay magistrate' is no longer used in practice because:

- even though magistrates are volunteers, the level and quality of public service which they provide is nowadays of a high 'professional' standard rather than of a purely 'amateur' nature

- there is no longer any need to use the term 'lay' to differentiate them from their full-time, legally-qualified, paid colleagues who used to be called 'stipendiary magistrates' but who are now called 'district judges' (or to use the full title 'district judge (magistrates' courts)').

Being a magistrate provides an opportunity for the ordinary (non-legally qualified) person to join the 30,000 or so existing magistrates, all themselves ordinary members of the public, who already deliver a large part of criminal and civil justice in England and Wales.

Strictly speaking, there is no longer any need for magistrates to be British nationals, or 'citizens' of the UK, although they will need to show that they have permanent ties to England and Wales and take an oath of allegiance to the sovereign before they can take up the position of JP.

NOTE: Although Scotland has justices of the peace, their role and functions are very different and the system is administered totally separately.

The system in England and Wales is, then, very much about society itself delivering justice rather than it being done on its behalf. The 'job' is obviously very demanding but is expressly accessible to the widest possible range of people.

The term 'job' has been used here even though this is a voluntary, part-time, unpaid role (save for limited expenses).

If you are appointed as a magistrate the demands on you to show commitment, professionalism and take part in continuing development will be not unlike those in any full-time, paid role. This said, the benefits to you (and possibly your employer) can be considerable, for, not only will you be providing an essential public service, but you will also be learning and developing in such valuable areas as:

- working as part of a team

- recognising and avoiding bias, prejudice, discrimination and stereotyping

- structured decision-making

- giving reasons for decisions

- communication skills

- time management

- accepting responsibility

- leadership, mentoring and appraisal

- assimilating and processing large amounts of detailed information.

This guide will then:

- help you to decide if the 'job' is right for you

- help you to gain and/or research the information you need to know before you consider applying by 'Checking Out the Territory'

- guide you through the application process

- tell you what attributes are being looked for by the Advisory Committees who recommend applicants to the Lord Chancellor for appointment

- give you some idea of the kind of questions that might be asked of you in interview

- give you some idea of the things you might need to ask yourself

- help you to prepare for interview and present yourself in your most positive light

- give you some idea of what your early days on the bench will involve

- emphasise the 'career nature' of what you will be letting yourself in for by telling you what further opportunities might arise once you are 'on the bench'.

The information in this guide is provided so that you can make informed decisions and comments based on your own life and circumstances rather than just supplying 'stock answers'. This is particularly important, since those who appoint magistrates are looking for people who possess specific qualities, which cannot be learned 'parrot fashion'. What this guide will encourage you to do is to:

- work out for yourself whether you have those qualities;

and

- suggest how best you can demonstrate them during the appointments process.

In any event, should you seek to enter a role for which you are not suited, or equally one that is not suited to you, then nobody benefits. This is really all part and parcel of one particular quality on which you might wish to focus, that of integrity. The integrity you will be expected to display as a magistrate in court should shine through in your application and the answers you give at your interviews. Despite the effort

that you will be required to put into the role you should know that many magistrates obtain a great deal of satisfaction from their duties and also the sort of reward (even enjoyment) that comes from working with equally committed colleagues and doing an important job well. Existing magistrates will want to know that an equally committed person who cares about what they are doing is about to join their ranks.

You will be encouraged to know that magistrates come from all walks of life and not discouraged just because you think that you do not fit some (probably misleading) 'stereotype'. Diversity is valued and sought after. What matters is your sound judgement in everyday situations, not whether you look like a magistrate from 'central casting'! In other words be yourself.

You should note that, if appointed, you will generally deal only with adult crime cases (i.e. allegations against defendants aged 18 years and over) and some other forms of criminal and civil work. Youth and family work (and the possibility also of sitting alongside a judge on appeals in the Crown Court) follow later, when you are more experienced.

Good luck in your research and application.

The how2become team

How2Become Team

CHAPTER 2
IS THE 'JOB' FOR YOU?

It might already have struck you that becoming a magistrate is a bit like marriage ('not to be entered into lightly') or taking on an animal ('for life, not just for Xmas'!). Although the Lord Chancellor will look for a minimum period of service of five years, it is an activity that will probably occupy you for many years to come. So you should think medium to long term. Many magistrates continue right up to their 70th birthday (which is when retirement usually occurs). This is again something to bear in mind during the application process and you should be prepared to let it be known that you understand the considerable demands that will be made on you.

Furthermore, if early retirement from the bench later becomes necessary, length of service may be one of the relevant factors as to whether or not the magistrate concerned will be recommended to go onto the Supplemental List and thereby continue to use the suffix 'JP'. So it's very important that you appreciate at the outset what you are letting yourself in for (and possibly your family and employer as well). Having a fully informed appreciation of the above will not only prevent

 how2become

any problems further down the line but will also enable you to deal well at interview with at least one of the 'Six Key Qualities' that are being sought in a candidate, that of 'Commitment' (which we will consider again later).

Recruitment or other publicity may suggest that your basic commitment will be:

- 26 half-days sittings a year
- some (reasonably substantial) initial and then continuing training
- attending the occasional bench meeting.

On one level this is correct, but it masks factors such as:

- sticking with the dates which you will have agreed in advance as those when you will attend court: you should only cancel your sitting at the last moment in a real emergency (the court must still run and replacement magistrates are not always available at short notice)
- cancelled sittings (which you will need to make up)
- cases that go 'part-heard' to another day (when you may need to come back to court for an extra sitting)
- contested hearings that last for more than half a day, possibly several days
- special hearings of various kinds
- full day lists of cases
- the wider contributions you might care to make to the role, e.g. sitting on bench committees, (later on) youth or family work or sitting on appeals at the Crown Court, and becoming a mentor to or appraiser of a JP colleague or two.

Although your application to become a magistrate will not be rejected merely because you can (initially at least) only offer the 'bare minimum' of 26 half days, experience shows that, if you pitch your commitment solely at this level then:

- you may often be struggling to meet your 26 half-day sittings if some have been cancelled and you cannot then make them up ad hoc (some magistrates will even use paid holiday from work on occasions to keep their sittings up).

- you will find it harder to acquire, maintain and demonstrate on appraisal the formal competences required of magistrates (please see later).

- you may be unable to play a full part in the life of the bench.

- you may even feel somewhat on the sidelines and out of touch if your JP colleagues are more experienced, involved and active in the affairs of the bench.

However, if you are appointed:

- attempts will be made (as far as consistent with the work and your need to sit on a range of work) to accommodate your personal circumstances (e.g. teachers preferring to sit in school holidays or parents of young children preferring to sit in term time) but do not assume that this will always be feasible or desirable.

- you will usually sit 'in threes' (but not always, although never in greater numbers).

- you will usually use a formal structured decision-making process (which you will learn about during your training so that it may also be useful to think about this kind of decision-making and at the very least to recognise the

terminology: broadly it means taking decisions in stages, one step at a time and considering all relevant matters at each stage before moving on to the next one).

- you will have access to national guidelines on matters such as sentencing. There is now a national Sentencing Guidelines Council (SGC) and you can access the SGC website at the address given at the end of this guide. Do not expect to learn everything before your interview. But knowing just a little about how sentencing works may help you to show serious interest.

- there is a rule of 'collective responsibility' i.e. if a consensus does not emerge, the bench will reach a majority decision and that will be deemed to be the decision of the bench as a whole and as if they were all in agreement. Publicly, there will be no indication of dissention or qualification. So you need to know how to act with discretion.

- you will draw up then, via your court chairman colleague, collective, public reasons for virtually all your decisions on the bench. So be prepared to show that you understand the importance of processes of reasoning and to be outvoted in private on occasions without getting concerned (unless of course it happens all the time!).

- but be aware that decisions of your bench may not always find favour with the public or press (or even family or friends) and you will usually not be able to go behind the reasons given publicly in court in an attempt to justify your position to your personal friends and acquaintances.

- you and your bench colleagues will work as a team along with your professionally qualified legal adviser who can

(and has the duty and right) to advise you on matters of law, practice, procedure, drafting reasons, etc but not on matters of pure fact or (subject to legal provisions) the actual sentence you may chose to impose.

- you will, initially with the help of a mentor, seek to become proficient in three competences (as they are known): 'Managing Yourself', 'Teamwork' and 'Making Judicial Decisions'.

- a trained colleague will, at least every three years, help you through an appraisal process on these competences.

But don't be put off by the extent of the above.

If you looked too closely at most activities in life you would never try anything new or interesting! So, with the benefit of a realistic idea about what might be involved in becoming a magistrate, let's move on to consider the typical work of a magistrates' court so that, if called for interview, you will able to provide sound and sensible answers, based on your own knowledge, experience or research.

SOME THINGS TO DO

- Make a quick initial, informal observation at your local magistrates' court (note that other, formal observations will be needed later). There is no need at this stage to 'book' in for this. Magistrates' courts are open to the public. But there is no harm and nothing lost in telling the usher (in the black gown) why you are there and he or she may help you in other ways depending on local practice).

- Think how you will manage your personal, family and working life so as to be able to meet the time commitment when you are a magistrate?

- Think even harder and make sure you are prepared to take on such extensive duties.

- Consider whether you are prepared to meet some of the other commitments of being a magistrate described above.

- Consider whether you need to make any more initial enquiries.

CHAPTER 3
OVERVIEW OF A MAGISTRATE'S DUTIES

All magistrates, from initial appointment, will sit on what is generally known as the 'adult bench'. This is through what is known as a nationwide 'Commission of the Peace' which means, for instance that:

- Work can be moved across areas.

- Magistrates can, on occasions, be asked to sit in neighbouring areas, say to help out if there is a temporary recruitment problem.

- If magistrates move areas the process of 'transfer' may be relatively easy.

- The selection and training will be roughly the same across England and Wales.

However, on appointment, all magistrates are assigned to a 'local justice area' for operational and pastoral purposes.

This will usually be the court area nearest to your home or, if different, nearest to your place of work (as requested by you on application: so think about this).

The **adult bench** deals with work such as:

- Criminal proceedings against people aged 18 years and over.

- Criminal proceedings against corporate bodies, companies, shops, etc.

- Applications for anti-social behaviour orders ('ASBOs').

- Remand hearings: whether someone should be given bail or held in custody.

- Search warrants and warrants of entry to premises.

- Miscellaneous civil work.

Magistrates will become versed in both equality and fairness considerations and in particular those which flow from the Human Rights Act 1998, so think about why protecting people's rights in this way is important. The 1998 Act is meant to be a safeguard against tyranny and abuse which can set in through lax standards as shown by events around the world.

Magistrates and judges make up 'The Judiciary'. The Judiciary is one of the 'arms of state' (but an arm which is independent from the other two, the Government (or Executive) and Parliament (or Legislature). The courts come under the Ministry of Justice through HM Court Service. But only for administrative purposes. Magistrates and judges are independent of both. As a magistrates you will have the power, in effect, to:

- confiscate people's money

- confiscate their property

- restrict their liberty

- remove their liberty altogether

- intervene in other people's family life

- decide where children should live

- decide where children should not live

- remove children from certain surroundings.

It is, therefore, vitally important before you attend any interview that you consider matters such as **fairness, equality, bias, prejudice, discrimination, stereotyping, human rights** and so on and think about how you might explain your feelings on such matters if they come up at interview.

For example, why do you know, or think that you can act without bias or prejudice? Has crime affected you or someone you know so that you can speak from experience, but in a balance way taking into account any competing points of view? Are you aware of the facts as opposed to rumour, speculation or media sensationalism? What are the real crime issues in your community?

The procedural and technical aspects of court work can be taught to most people but your basic underlying values and understanding is harder to change. Your way of looking at things can and will be enhanced by training and exposure to the many different kinds of views that you will find amongst your JP colleagues.

As far as adult offenders are concerned, there are three broad types of criminal offence:

There are some absolute bars to appointment such as:

- you are under 18 years of age

- you are aged 70 years or over (see below if you are aged 65 or over)

- your health will prevent you from carrying out the duties properly (but see below regarding disabilities)

- by inference, you will not be appointed if you do not either live or work in England and Wales (although as stated earlier your nationality is no longer a factor)

- you are seeking asylum or hold a Sector Based Scheme Visa

- you are a serving police officer, special constable, prison service employee, traffic warden, probation officer, bailiff, member of the Crown Prosecution Service (CPS) staff or directly involved in law enforcement

- you are an employee of the NSPCC or RSPCA (both of whom regularly bring cases to court).

NOTE: The above list is far from exhaustive and may, on occasions, be capable of special adaptation.

You should check with the guidance for applicants and/or your local Advisory Committee (see the section 'Getting Started On and Submitting Your Application') if you (or a spouse, partner or close relative) is in any way closely involved with any activity connected with magistrates' courts which might possibly give rise to a potential conflict of interest.

Although being 65 years or over is not an automatic bar to appointment, in practice the selection and training process can be fairly lengthy and the Lord Chancellor would normally expect at least five years' service before retirement from the bench occurs at aged 70 years.

There are many other personal factors that may or may not affect the likelihood of you appointment which the Advisory Committee will need to evaluate.

These could, for instance, include:

• if you are a solicitor or barrister

NOTE: You will recall that having a legal qualification is definitely not a prerequisite to appointment. Conversely, possessing one is not itself an aid to appointment or a disqualification.

• some civil servants

• some employees of local authorities

• some members of the armed forces

• social workers, care managers, education welfare officers, ministers of religion

• interpreters

• licensees of public houses

• bookmakers

• lay visitors to police stations or prisons

• MPs, MEPs, members of the Welsh assembly and full-time party political agents.

NOTE: Again, the above list is far from exhaustive and will require particular consideration by the Advisory Committee. You should check with the guidance for applicants and/or your local Advisory Committee (see the section 'Getting Started On and Submitting Your Application') if you (or a spouse, partner or close relative) is in any way closely involved with any activity which might potentially give rise to a conflict of interest.

Advisory Committees will, however, be keen to steer a proper way through such issues whenever possible, especially if you could be appointed to an area away from where you undertake activities which might otherwise be in conflict.

A special word on **criminal convictions** (yours or those of a spouse, partner, close family member or close friend):

- whereas magistrates obviously have to possess integrity (above), command the respect of others and generally be of good character, the existence of criminal convictions need not, of itself, preclude appointment

- this will be covered in greater detail later under 'The Six Key Qualities' and 'Getting Started On and Submitting Your Application'.

As for **health** and **disabilities** (including sight impairment), these will initially not be relevant unless they would clearly prevent you carrying out the duties of a magistrate. Any applicant with a disability should initially be assessed solely against the 'Six Key Qualities' and without reference to the disability (save for any issues around where and how any interview is to be held). Should appointment ultimately appear appropriate, only then will issues around the possibility of 'reasonable adjustments' be considered and as a quite separate matter.

SOME THINGS TO DO

- Check any issues around your eligibility for appointment, especially if you have any doubts about it.

- Check the guidance for applicants that comes with the application form (see later under 'Getting Started On and Submitting Your Application').

CHAPTER 5
DO YOU HAVE THE 'SIX KEY QUALITIES'?

Advisory Committees on the Appointment of Magistrates must assess applicants against what are known as the 'Six Key Qualities'. These are set out in the notes accompanying application forms and are as follows:

1. GOOD CHARACTER

What type of character do you think you need to have in order to become a magistrate? You must be honest and possess a high level of integrity. Before you are offered a position as magistrate the assessing panel will ask for references. Each reference that you provide must be capable of vouching for your character. It is no use stating that you are honest, and a person of integrity, if it is not true. Your current or previous employer will usually be able to vouch for your character. As you can imagine, you must be able to respect confidentiality.

Magistrates need to be trusted individuals as they are privy to much confidential information. It would not be acceptable as a magistrate to discuss cases or confidential information with your friends, family or strangers. As a magistrate you are trusted not to bring the magistracy into disrepute.

Consider the following key areas of this quality before making your application:

- Personal integrity

- Respect and trust of others

- Respect for confidences

- Absence of any matter which might bring them or the magistracy into disrepute

- Willingness to be circumspect in private, working and public life.

2. UNDERSTANDING AND COMMUNICATION

Magistrates must be able to communicate effectively both in writing and verbally. They must also have a strong ability to understand, read and interpret written documents, and also extract relevant facts that will assist them in dealing with the case in hand. Throughout the selection process you will be assessed on your ability to achieve this important personal quality.

Consider the following key areas of this quality before making your application:

- Ability to understand documents

- Identify and comprehend relevant facts

- Follow evidence and arguments

- Ability to concentrate

- Ability to communicate effectively

3. SOCIAL AWARENESS

Having an understanding of society is crucial to the role of a magistrate. You must also understand and have respect for diversity and people from different cultures and social backgrounds. Ask yourself the following question – "Do I understand my local community?" If the answer is yes, then you are well on the way to being capable of demonstrating this quality during the selection process. If the answer is no, then now is the right time to learn. Take a look at the following definition of diversity:

'The concept of diversity encompasses acceptance and respect. It means understanding that each individual is unique, and recognising our individual differences. These can be along the dimensions of race, ethnicity, gender, sexual orientation, socio-economic status, age, physical abilities, religious beliefs, political beliefs, or other ideologies. It is the exploration of these differences in a safe, positive, and nurturing environment. It is about understanding each other and moving beyond simple tolerance to embracing and celebrating the rich dimensions of diversity contained within each individual.'

Consider the following key areas of this quality before making your application:

- Appreciation and acceptance of the Rule of Law (this is the fundamental principle that no one is above the law and that everyone is subject to it in equal measure)

- Understanding of society in general

 how2become

- Respect for people from different ethnic, cultural or social backgrounds (and maybe some knowledge of 'other communities')

- Awareness and understanding of life beyond family, friends and work is highly desirable

- As is an understanding of your local community.

4. MATURITY AND SOUND TEMPERAMENT

All magistrates must have a good level of maturity and temperament. They must be capable of working with other people on a professional basis and understand that everybody has differing opinions. They must have respect for other people and their differences and be able to reach agreed solutions to problems. They must also be assertive when required, decisive and confident, be fair and have respect and courtesy for everyone.

Consider the following key areas of this quality before making your application:

- Ability to relate to and work with others

- Regard for the views of others

- Willingness to consider advice

- Humanity, firmness, decisiveness, confidence, a sense of fairness, courtesy.

5. SOUND JUDGEMENT

As a magistrate you must be capable of making sound judgements that are not based on your own personal feelings, prejudices or biased opinions. For example, if

you have personally been the victim of burglary or theft previously, how would you feel if an offender was in front of you for a similar offence? Would you be inclined to pass down a tougher sentence, simply because you have been a victim before? Obviously the answer should be no and you should never be influenced by such external factors when sentencing individuals. Your judgements must be based on the facts of the case and also on your ability to think logically, objectively and with an open mind.

Consider the following key areas of this quality before making your application:

- Ability to think logically, weigh arguments and reach a balanced decision

- Openness of mind, objectivity, the recognition of and controlling of prejudices.

6. COMMITMENT AND RELIABILITY

Because magistrates are not paid a salary then the role requires a high level of commitment and motivation. You need to be motivated for different reasons other than financial gain. A commitment to serve the community is obviously a must and you will be assessed against this desire during the selection process. If you have already worked within the community previously then this can work in your favour. Any form of voluntary work will demonstrate to the assessors that you are committed and motivated by other reasons other than financial reward.

For many people, the thought of becoming a magistrate is extremely appealing. However, once they start to carry out the role they soon realise that it requires a high level of commitment for sustained period of time. Make sure that

you are fully aware of the commitment required to become a magistrate before you apply.

Why do you think you need to be reliable in order to become a magistrate? In the build up to court proceedings, a date and time for the case to be heard will be set. This can be weeks in advance. Therefore, it is crucial that you can be relied upon to commit to specific times and dates. Unless there is very good reason, such as illness or otherwise, you will not be able to phone in and cancel your attendance in court. It is extremely important that you can be relied upon to provide the minimum number of sittings per year. Whilst on this subject, you are required to commit to at least 26 half day sittings per year. That equates to one half day sitting every fortnight which is usually acceptable to most people.

In addition to the commitment to court sittings you must also be able to commit to the training that is required to become a competent magistrate.

Consider the following key areas of this quality before making your application:

- Reliability, commitment to serve the community, willingness to undertake at least 26 half day sittings a year (but possibly more in practice as mentioned earlier: although that is for your own information and you will not be pressed on it at this stage to commit above the basic requirement)

- Willingness to undertake the required training

- Ability to offer the requisite time

- Support of family and employer

- Sufficiently good health.

For most practical purposes these will be the only matters that Advisory Committees are required and permitted to assess. In the later sections on 'First Interview' and 'Second Interview' we will consider how and when the Advisory Committees assess these qualities and how you might best prepare yourself to give a demonstrably considered reply at interview.

Both in the application form and at both interviews you will also be asked what used to be called the 'Key Question' but is now known as the 'Good Character and Background Question':

Is there anything in your private or working life or in your past, or to your knowledge in that of any member of your family or close friends, which, if it became generally known, might bring you or the magistracy into disrepute, or call into question your integrity, authority or standing as a magistrate?

Again, we will look at this question again when we consider the two interviews.

SOME THINGS TO DO

- Make sure that you are familiar with all aspects of the Six Key Qualities and how you might demonstrate them at interview as part of your general approach to things that you may be asked about.

- Consider how you will answer the 'Good Character and Background Question' (you might end up answering it on three separate occasions).

- Consider the three competences and whether you are ready, after appointment and following training etc, for the process of being appraised on these.

CHAPTER 6
CHECKING OUT THE TERRITORY

It has already been mentioned that at an early stage you should pay an informal visit to your local magistrates' court. This will give you various opportunities, including:

- to see what life in a magistrates' court is really like

- to observe the wide range of people who are doing the job already

- to get to know the kind of cases that magistrates' deal with

- to appreciate the solemnity and 'rituals' of court proceedings

- to soak up the atmosphere in general.

There are other sources of preliminary investigation. These include:

- the public library (one very useful introduction to

magistrates' courts is mentioned at the end of this guide and is also available from How2Become)

- the internet (a note of useful sites appears at the end of this introduction)

- friends and acquaintances who may be magistrates (but beware trying to cultivate influence: you must stand on your own application, commitment and knowledge)

- friends and acquaintances who may be practitioners within the Criminal Justice System and who may have regular contact with the magistrates' court or know of its work

- friends and acquaintances who may have appeared in court as defendants, witnesses or who may have been victims of crime and who can tell you of their own experience, and how they felt about the way they were treated

- people in the community who work with crime prevention initiatives and the like.

None of this early 'recognisance' will be wasted if you decide to proceed with an application as your sense of what magistrates' courts are all about will be developing all the time as you begin to follow the instructions for formal observation at court which you will find in the application pack.

It will also help you to build social and judicial awareness of the role of the magistrate. Equipped with this guide and knowledge of the 'Six Key Qualities' you will be able to think about and see how these connect to day to day events which again will be of considerable value when it comes to your later interviews.

THE COMPETENCE FRAMEWORK

Allied to some aspects of the key qualities is the issue of the magistrates' Competences Framework, which, as already noted above, covers:

- 'Managing Yourself'

- 'Teamwork'

- 'Making Judicial Decisions'

Although you will receive far more information about this in initial training, Advisory Committees may, nevertheless, wish to discuss such matters at interview when looking at the Six Key Qualities, so some broad, initial awareness of these matters on your part would be useful.

As with 'Checking Out the Territory', the better informed you are the more this will be likely to come over at interview; and is also likely to give you greater confidence in answering questions.

CHAPTER 7
SOME 'INSIDER' TIPS BEFORE YOU START

Within this section of the guide we have provided you with some very important insider tips that will help you to pass the selection process. Follow them carefully and your chances of success will dramatically increase.

TIP I
Always be yourself during the selection process
The interview process is not a traditional competitive one as at a job interview – Advisory Committees are positively looking to involve as many appropriate people as possible as magistrates and from a range of backgrounds.

So, try to relax and just give the best account of yourself that you can. What is likely to impress the Advisory Committee most is the 'real you' and whether that person possesses certain qualities. It is important that your own qualities come through rather than some polished 'performance' geared to

the occasion, or worse trying to 'beat the system' by second guessing what you think that the Advisory Committee would like to hear! Remember that Advisory Committees are trained and experienced in dealing with people and sensing the genuine article.

Even experienced magistrates learn something new every day. Don't feel the need to present as virtually the 'ready made article', having researched all the technical aspects of becoming a magistrate; the Advisory Committees will essentially just be looking for how well you demonstrate the Six Key Qualities.

TIP 2
Check the minimum eligibility requirements first
If an applicant is not obviously ineligible a first interview will often be offered as a matter of course. So, do spend some time on making sure that you have read all the accompanying notes to the application form and have completed it fully and as required. We will look later at some of the specific questions on the application form.

Pay particular attention to the need to have observed a court sitting before submitting your application and the advice about 'Checking Out the Territory' above (and see also Tip 9 below)

TIP 3
The six key qualities
Have ready for interview examples from your own life experiences to help to demonstrate the Six Key Qualities. During the interview you will be asked questions that relate to the key qualities. Here are a few examples to help you get started:

> **Q.** Can you explain how you intend to be committed to the role and requirements of a magistrate?

Q. Please give an example of where you have been committed and reliable in a previous job or role.

Q. Tell us what you understand about the community in which you are living? What problems does it face?

Q. Tell us why you are of good character? How would other people describe you?

TIP 4

Be aware of the assessable criteria

You need to be aware of how the Six Key Qualities are assessed.

'Good Character' and 'Commitment' will be assessed as either 'demonstrated' or 'not demonstrated'. So, with no shades of grey, you need give these two direct consideration.

The other four Qualities are 'scored' and assessed as:

Level 0 = not demonstrated: little or no positive evidence

Level 1 = demonstrated: generally positive

Level 2 = well demonstrated: positive evidence

Level 3 = very well demonstrated: very strong evidence

There is no higher or minimum overall 'score' required in respect of each of these four Qualities just as long as you demonstrate at least Level 1 in each of them. You will then be eligible for appointment, on the basis that your attributes can be developed/enhanced later through training, mentoring and appraisal.

However:

• you are somewhat vulnerable if the best you aim to score is Level 1 in all four Qualities as you may not then be 'held over' as described below

- should there be many more candidates actual vacancies then generally those with the highest overall 'scores' will usually be selected (although those with lower scores will usually be held over against any future need)

TIP 5
Think carefully about where you want to sit

Advisory Committees usually work in annual recruitment cycles (although some very large areas may recruit more often and some very small areas less often).

If you enquire of the Advisory Committee(s) in respect of the areas where you live and work (see 'Getting Started and Submitting Your Application') you should be able to discover which is recruiting when and also where the greatest number of vacancies might be. This may help you to decide where to apply and how to time your application (i.e. speed it up if necessary or perhaps hold it back for a time and submit it on the basis of known, up-to-date recruitment requirements).

Decide which area it might be better for you to carry out your sittings as a magistrate – near to home or near to work (assuming they are in different areas).

List the pros and cons of each, based on factors such as ease of attending court, training and meetings, effect on home and social life, which area might be recruiting earlier or have more vacancies etc.

If you are willing to sit at either location, then mention this on your application form and submit your application to whichever area you feel is most appropriate in your particular circumstances.

TIP 6
Be open and honest from the beginning and do not hide anything!

If you think there may be issues around potential disqualifi-

cation (e.g. because of your work or that of close relatives) then seek the advice of the Advisory Committee secretary as early in the process as possible.

The same applies if you think you may have issues around answering the 'Good Character and Background' question – it's far better to be told at the outset that there may probably nothing to worry about than to fail to mention an issue and then later for you to say that you thought that it was not relevant.

This may be viewed as evidence of poor judgment or a lack of integrity rather than openness and honesty. **Knowing what is and is not relevant** in any given situation is part and parcel of being a magistrate.

TIP 7
Convictions and cautions

Again, if you have any significant previous convictions or cautions (formal warnings by the police), the secretary may be able to offer you some initial guidance – but always disclose them fully at all times.

In any event, in respect of previous convictions, be prepared at interview to provide information such as:

• the full circumstances

• your views and feelings on matters such as the prosecution process, the court process, the sentence

• how the outcome affected your views on law and order.

Remember that, in the case of all applicants who are to be appointed, an enhanced Criminal Records Bureau (CRB) check will be made. So deal with any issues around previous convictions head-on and at the outset.

TIP 8
Complete the application with the 6 key qualities in mind
In completing your application form and in preparing for and attending at interview keep the Six Key Qualities very much to the fore of your mind and make sure that you have thought about how you might provide examples which are consistent with these, both from your own life and also in answer to the questions and exercises that will be coming your way (more on these later).

TIP 9
Court visits
When you come to do the required, formal pre-application court observations:

- these should be in one of the 'adult crime courts' (ask the usher if you are in doubt: look for the one with the 'best spread of cases')

- don't just go for the suggested minimum of one visit to court – two or three will show commitment, give you more to talk about at interview and also give you a real idea of what the 'job' really entails (You may find it more interesting than you thought. If not, nothing is lost since you might want to re-assess whether you are really doing the right thing)

- also, for much the same reasons, try to stay as long as possible on each day: unusual and instructive things can happen at any moment

- with these visits geared to your application you do really need to check in advance with the court office rather than rely on the 'open court' principle already mentioned, in order to see what days are best (the staff will be used accommodating such observations and making sure that

you see a spread of cases). See, particularly, if you can observe **remand, trial** and **sentencing** courts.

- ask if the court office or usher can provide you with a copy court list so that you can follow matters better and make notes more easily

- without 'making a nuisance of yourself', or appearing 'too keen', use any reasonable opportunity to ask questions of staff on the day (or of magistrates if that opportunity arises: some courts do facilitate this but you should follow whatever the local practice is)

- make some notes on the day and keep them for the interview so you can refer back to what you observed and, perhaps, even more importantly, what your thoughts and feelings were about what you saw.

TIP 10
Consider community or voluntary work
Voluntary work or other work in the community is not a prerequisite to appointment (and may, on occasions, have to be given up on appointment if there is any potential conflict of interest: see earlier). But it is a useful route to demonstrating 'Key Qualities' such as 'Commitment' and 'Social Awareness'.

Otherwise (and in any event), be ready at interview to demonstrate how you, in other ways, gain and possess social awareness.

TIP 11
Think about the reasons why you want to become a magistrate
Consider why you really want to become a magistrate – this will arise on the application form and also at interview. 'Putting something back into the community' is a common

reason given but you will (and must) have your own reasons and explanation as to how you think you will do this by being a magistrate.

With most of the questions you will be asked there is no 'set answer' or 'expected answer'. You need to demonstrate that you can think and respond as the interview develops (as you would have to do in court), especially perhaps in terms of giving reasons for what you say. 'Putting something back' may well be a genuine reason, but be ready to say why you have chosen this particular route above any others available to you.

All this has to come from you. Wanting to 'fight crime', 'help those who feel they have to resort to crime' or 'because it's a noble office' are probably not good reasons – being a magistrate is about service and applying the law as it exists and balancing the interests of all involved according to legal and guideline provisions. So avoid being 'a knight (or dame) in shining armour', a vigilante who wants to put the world to rights (people have been striving for centuries and around the world to find complete or tidy answers to crime) and recognise that you will be entering a world in which **due process**, the **Rule of Law** (already mentioned) and principles of **fairness** and **justice** are uppermost.

You might like to think of the oath that you will be required to take if and when you are appointed which seems to say quite a lot:

'I will well and truly serve our Sovereign Lady Queen Elizabeth the Second, in the office of Justice of the Peace and will do right to all manner of people after the laws and usages of the Realm without fear or favour, affection or ill-will'.

Consider then also how you would respond if asked at interview if there any laws you feel should not exist (the old

'poll tax' used to be a good example and many people are involved in 'direct action' of one kind or another in pressing their campaigns or causes) and how you would feel if asked to apply 'unpopular laws' as a magistrate (see the Tip 17 below concerning the 'undertakings' that you will have to give in due course if and when appointed to the bench).

TIP 12
What can you bring to the magistracy?

Consider carefully how you will answer when asked (again, on the application form and at interview) what you will bring to the magistracy. Keep in mind the Six Key Qualities and think about your personal experiences and skills.

You may arrive at one or more of the following examples:

- appreciation of diverse backgrounds, lifestyles, etc

- preparedness to take on new duties with enthusiasm

- ability to balance potentially competing considerations

- ability to work in a team and accept collective responsibility

- a sense of fairness

- preparedness to work within structures and guidelines but still not losing sight of the individual features of the matter before you

- experience of meeting and dealing with a wide range of people

- knowing that there are 'two sides' to most arguments and that not all decisions are easy ones

- times when it may have been necessary for you to challenge people who have made inappropriate

remarks, especially those about people from marginal backgrounds or other people's lifestyles or preferences

- ability to stay calm, fair and unperturbed by things that may be said.

TIP 13
References

Choose your referees carefully and according to the guidance given. As one referee will usually be your employer, consider carefully who in your organisation that ought to be.

You will want them to be positive in what they say when the reference is taken up but you will also want them to support you in practical ways once appointed – so, it might pay to identify and consult them quite early on when you are thinking about applying to join the bench.

Although the Employment Rights Act 1996 provides for employees to take time off work to perform public duties, without suffering adverse reactions, such time does not have to be paid leave and is subject to a 'reasonableness test' which may have to be applied differently in different circumstances.

So, it's always best to discuss your intentions with your employer as early in the process as possible, reminding him or her of the skills you will acquire/enhance as a magistrate and will be able to bring back with you to the workplace.

The website www.businesslink.gov.uk (search against 'Time off for magistrate duties') may be of use in this respect.

TIP 14
Be fully prepared for the interviews

Consider the sections in this guide that relate to the two interviews and prepare carefully for the likely contents of

each one. There are some invaulable tips within the interview sections so make sure you follow them!

TIP 15
Interview tips
At each interview:

- the questioning will be probing but not intrusive so don't feel threatened or challenged by that next level of probing

- the interview panel (which will usually comprise three members, at least one of whom will not be a magistrate) will be trained to work with candidates who may not be used to interviews and will be trying by their questioning, amongst other things, to help you express yourself fully

- don't feel the need to show technical knowledge – just demonstrate the fact that you appreciate that you will need training and guidance

- but do show how you have arrived at your views and be ready to explain yourself and, if you are asked, enlarge on your conclusions

- remember that any interview is, to some extent, a two-way process so have a few meaningful questions of your own ready and, if they are all covered in interview, then say what they would have been but acknowledge that they have now been answered. Naturally, don't 'hi-jack' the interview by asking too many questions or otherwise demonstrate why you would be unlikely to make a sound magistrate! Again, keep thinking of the key qualities. It is perhaps better to relax and to concentrate on a few pertinent points rather than to be too 'spur of the moment' and risk a gush of poorly thought out questions one on top of other. Again, think about how in court you would have to be able to identify and go directly to the nub of whatever matter is under discussion.

TIP 16
Photocopy your application form before submitting it
Although at interview you will be offered sight of your application form, it is worth keeping your own copy:

- in case the original gets lost in the post on submission (see later)

- so that you can refresh your mind beforehand at your leisure rather than on the day

- so that you can be ready to deal with any significant subsequent changes when asked whether there are any since you made the application.

TIP 17
Undertakings and commitments
You need to be forewarned and ready to deal at any stage with the fact that, if later to be recommended for appointment, you will be required to provide undertakings which will include matters along the following lines:

- it will be your duty to administer justice according to the law

- you will be circumspect in your conduct and maintain the dignity, standing and good reputation of the magistracy at all times in your private, working and public life

- you will respect confidences

- you will complete all training which may, from time-to-time, be prescribed by the Lord Chancellor and will offer to resign if you fail to complete this training in the time specified without a reason acceptable to the Lord Chancellor

- you will sit for at least 26 half days each year and resign

if, without a reason acceptable to the Lord Chancellor, you fail to complete the minimum number of sittings

- you will resign if you become disqualified to sit as, or are unable to perform the duties of, a magistrate

- your actions as a magistrate will be free from any political, racial, sexual or other bias

- you will disclose any impending criminal or civil proceedings against you, or in which you become involved in any capacity, and the outcome and if disciplinary proceedings are taken against you by your employer or by a professional body or association

- if you become bankrupt or involved in any other financial difficulties or if a company, of which you are a director, goes into liquidation

- if a close relative (as defined in the Notes for Guidance that will be given to you with the application form) is involved in any criminal or civil proceedings and the outcome

- if you or a close relative (as defined in the Notes for Guidance) join the police force as a police officer, police community support officer or civilian or become a special constable, traffic warden, an employee of the Crown Prosecution Service (CPS), National Probation Service or HM Prison Service

- if you become or cease to be a freemason (see the guidance notes that accompany the application form in respect of freemasonry which is neither a bar nor a qualification but to which certain considerations attach)

- if you accept any position or office which would have disqualified you from appointment

Interviews will follow reasonably soon after the closing date for applications so check your dairy to make sure that you can be available and at fairly short notice and for both of them.

CHAPTER 8
GETTING STARTED AND PUTTING IN YOUR APPLICATION

Armed with the information that you've learnt so far, it's now time to get down to some practicalities and complete and submit your application.

You will need at least the following documentation:

- Application Form

- Application Form Guidance Notes

- A list of Advisory Committee Secretaries (see later for contact details)

- A knowledge of local magistrates' court areas, courthouses and locations.

The Ministry of Justice booklet 'Serving as a Magistrate' may also prove useful.

You can obtain these by various means, including often by enquiring at any magistrates' court or contacting local

Advisory Committee secretaries (whose details may have been in any recruitment publicity and who may well be based at or have direct links with local courthouses).

But you may find the following online resource the easiest and quickest method:

www.direct.gov.uk

This website, as its name suggests, is designed to give the public direct access to documentation and information such as the above without searching for it through various different departmental websites. You can follow the links through 'Crime, justice and the law' and then 'Becoming a magistrate' or just use the search box.

From this website you can either:

* download and print out an application form and then complete it by hand; or

* complete an 'interactive' application form online, print it off and then submit it in hard copy.

It is perhaps worth noting that the two types of application form above appear to have a slightly different format but both should cover exactly the same ground.

If you want the whole application pack in hard copy then either write to or e-mail:

The Magistrates' Appointment Team
Ministry of Justice
Magistrates Recruitment and Appointments Branch
Judicial Services Directorate
Room 5.40
5th Floor
102 Petty France
London SW1H 7AJ

E mail: mnrsteam@justice.gsi.gov.uk

The Ministry of Justice should also be able to provide essential parts of the paperwork in Braille. Complete the form fully, carefully and accurately (see the earlier 'Tips' section) and, as already suggested, keep your own copy. Failure to provide all information might delay your application or even prevent its being considered. Submit your completed form to the appropriate Advisory Committee secretary (i.e. the one for where you live or work as appropriate to your choice of area in which you would like to sit in court to hear cases).

Acknowledgement of receipt of your application should follow within five working days but make a note to check shortly after that and have your own copy to hand just in case you need to resubmit it. Once you know that your application has been received and that the recruitment process is under way then you need to start thinking about what the interviews might hold as in the next two sections of this guide.

Before we progress onto the interview stages of the selection process, we will now provide you with some information on how to complete the form in order to increase your chances of success.

HOW TO COMPLETE THE APPLICATION FORM

The application form is the first stage of the magistrates' selection process. The vast majority of applicants do not progress past this stage. Therefore it is crucial that give your application the time that it deserves. We strongly advise that you set aside at least two evenings during the week to complete the form using the guidance that has been provided within this guide, and also the guidance notes that

you will have received with your application pack. The first step in completing a successful application form is to read the 'guidance notes' carefully. Within the guidance notes you will receive some handy tips that will increase your chances of success.

MAKE SURE YOU ARE ELIGIBLE TO APPLY

The guidance notes will provide details of the criteria you must meet. Within the guidance notes there is also a section that relates to 'ineligibility criteria'. For obvious reasons, people who hold the position of Police Officer, Special Constable, Community Support Officer, Traffic Warden or Highways Agency Traffic Officer etc will not be eligible to apply. There are also further restrictions on employment positions contained within the guidance notes. If you have any doubts about the suitability of your occupation then we strongly advise that you contact the Local Advisory Committee for details and advice.

So, once you have successfully studied the application form guidance notes you can begin to complete your form. We advise that your first attempt at completing the form is done on a photocopied version. This will allow you to iron out any mistakes. If you are opting to complete the interactive version of the form then this will not be the case.

Important note – When completing the form use black ink, unless indicated otherwise. If a section of the form or a specific question does not apply to you it is important that you indicate this by inserting 'N/A' in the box provided. If you fail to do this then your application may be delayed. Do not leave the space or question blank, or even put a line through it. Remember, if you fail to follow simple instructions then your form may be delayed.

The first section of the form relates to 'personal information' and this is relatively simple to complete. Make sure your e mail address is readable as there have been many cases where an incorrect address has been provided, or it is unreadable. You will also be required to provide details of your educational qualifications. Only provide details of actual qualifications received as you may be required to supply evidence of these at the interview stage.

Once you have completed section 1 you will then move on to section 2 which is where you will provide details regarding your occupation. In order to complete this section you will need to have the guidance notes next to you so that you can relate to the relevant occupational groups. During section 2 you are required to provide details of your employer's business, or your own business if you are self employed. An example of this would be:

"My employer currently provides recruitment training courses and guides for the general public through the internet website www.how2become.co.uk. The contact details for the company include:

How2become Ltd
Suite 2
50 Churchill Square Business Centre
Kings Hill
Kent
ME19 4YU

The person for whom correspondence should be sent to is a Mr Ronald Fictitious. Telephone number 07890..."

You do not need to provide any further details than the above. If you are unsure as to the suitability of your employers business then we advise you contact the Local Advisory

Committee for guidance.

Following section 2 of the application form you will then be required to complete further sections that relate to details regarding your spouse/partner and relatives, details relating to criminal convictions or civil proceedings before eventually reaching the section where you have to state the reasons why you are applying to become a magistrate. Now obviously every section of the application form is important, but none more so than this. What you include within the following questions will determine whether or not your application is to be successful or not. Therefore you must take your time to construct strong answers.

Important note – under no circumstance are the following sample responses to be copied or used during any application to become a magistrate. They are to be used for guidance purposes only.

The first question relates to the reasons why you want to become a magistrate:

Question I

State the reasons why you want to become a magistrate.

Before you start to respond to this question write down in bullet points on a blank sheet of scrap paper exactly why you want to become a magistrate. Those applicants who provide reasons such as 'to put those people who offend away', or 'because it is a highly regarded position' will score little or no marks. In order to provide an accurate response to this question try to think about the role of a magistrate. Consider the following points:

• Magistrates hold a very important role that requires a high level of trust and integrity.

- They perform an essential 'public service'.

- The role requires a large amount of responsibility and commitment.

- Magistrates must have the ability to make sound judgements and decisions.

- They need to possess a high level of integrity.

- In order to perform their role competently they need to know their local community well.

- They must ensure that people in society are treated fairly.

- You do not need a legal background but they must have a high level of common sense.

Now take a look at the following sample response to this question:

Sample Response to Question I

"Over the last three years I have had the opportunity to carry out voluntary work within the community. This has been in the form of working at my local community centre for a few hours per week. I have learnt a tremendous amount during that time and it has opened my eyes to my local community. I want to become a magistrate because I very much enjoy working in the community and the skills and experiences I have gained through my voluntary work would be very much suited to this role.

I understand that the role of a magistrate is one that requires a high level of responsibility, coupled with the ability to make sound judgements and decisions. I have held numerous management positions during my career and I have very much enjoyed the responsibilities I have been entrusted with. I see the role of a magistrate to be very similar in that you

are required to act with a high degree of integrity, trust and maturity and I have always excelled in these types of roles."

You will see from the above sample response that the person has a genuine desire to work in a role that is focused on the community. The applicant has also made reference to the type of role a magistrate performs and he has also tried to match his skills and experiences with some of the more prominent qualities of a magistrate.

Now take a look at question 2

Question 2

What qualities do you believe you could bring to the magistracy?

This question should be relatively easy to respond to, providing you have the qualities required to become a magistrate. Before we provide a sample response to this question let us first of all re-cap on the type of qualities a magistrate is required to have:

The qualities of a magistrate

- Be of sound character;

- Possess a high level of integrity;

- Respect confidentiality;

- Trusted;

- Committed, motivated and reliable;

- A commitment to serve the community;

- The ability to make sound judgements;

- Communicate effectively both in writing and verbally;

- Have an understanding of society;

- Respect diversity and people from different cultures and social backgrounds;

- Maturity and temperament.

Once you are aware of the relevant qualities that the role of a magistrate involves, you will then be able to respond to the question in an accurate manner. It is important that you only provide details of 'actual' qualities you possess as you will be further questioned on these if you are invited to interview.

Now take a look at the sample response to this question:

Sample Response to Question 2

"Through my voluntary work in the community I believe I can bring a high level of respect for everyone in society regardless of their background or appearance. I have a strong ability to make judgements based on facts and common sense. Within my work and home life I am a respected person and I have always had the ability to listen to people carefully and not make decisions on first appearances, as these are often inaccurate. I am reliable, committed and motivated and have a clear understanding of the local community and more importantly its needs. Finally, I am a mature person who can listen to other peoples view points before making decisions. I believe the skills that I have provided within this application form are just a few of the positive aspects I could bring to the magistracy team."

It is worth mentioning at this point that you are more than likely going to be asked questions at the interview stage that relate to the responses you provide on the application form. Therefore, it is crucial that you photocopy your form before you send it of. For example, in response we provided you in question 2 it states:

"I believe the skills that I have provided within this application form are just a few of the positive aspects I could bring to the magistracy team."

It is quite feasible that during the interview stage the panel will ask the applicant what other 'positive aspects' they could bring to the magistracy team. Make sure you can answer questions that are based around your application form. There may also be a question on the application form that relates to your experiences of voluntary or community. If you have never been involved in any voluntary or community work then we strongly advise that you do so. This will be a big plus during your application and it provides genuine evidence that you have the interests of your community at heart. There are numerous ways that you can become involved in voluntary work or community work such as working in a charity shop, or devoting time to your local community centre.

We will now provide you with a sample response to the type of question that relates to your involvement with community or voluntary work.

Question 3

Have you been, or are you currently involved, in any form of voluntary work in your local community or otherwise?

"At various times during my life I have been involved in community and voluntary work, something which I gain a tremendous amount from.

I currently help out at my local community centre for 2 hours a week. This involves helping the other members of the team get the centre ready for forthcoming events and also making the tea for the over 60's group which comes in on Wednesday mornings.

In addition to this work I have also spent a 3 month period working 1 day a week at my local charity shop. Whilst this was approximately 5 years ago I still gained a huge amount of experience whilst mixing with and communicating with different members of the community.

Finally, I organised a charity fun day at my child's local school in order to raise money for some new computer equipment for the children. This was a great success and we all managed to raise £1400 for the good cause."

On the application form within the section that relates to your reasons for wanting to become a magistrate you may also get asked to detail you spare time activities and interests. The question may appear like this:

Question 4

Please provide details of what you do in your spare time in relation to your interests and activities.

Questions of this nature are designed to assess what you do outside of work and the type of things you are involved in. For example, if you say that you are 'out socialising with you're your mates every weekend' or that you 'spend a lot of time on the computer searching the internet' then you will not score highly. They want to see that you are a settled and rounded person, someone who is stable, mature and reliable.

Take a look at the following sample response to this question.

Sample Response to Question 4

Please provide details of what you do in your spare time in relation to your interests and activities.

"I am very much a stable family person who enjoys the spare time I have with my wife and children. We always try to plan activities months in advance and often take the children away on activity weekends when possible. In addition to my family life I am a keen sportsperson who plays golf and cricket for local teams. I can also often be seen running very early in the morning before going to work. In addition to my fitness activities I am currently involved in a period of self development and have embarked on a distance learning course in creative writing which I very much enjoy."

There will then follow two questions that relate to any previous magistrate applications you have submitted and which magistrate's court you have visited. As we have stated previously within this guide it is crucial that you visit at least one magistrates court, preferably the one you want to sit at. If you do not visit a magistrate's court then you are unlikely to be invited to attend the first interview.

The final few sections of the application form will then relate to your health and disability, a good character declaration and references. During the insider tips and advice section we indicated how important it was to provide suitable references. You will see from the form that you are required to provide details of three references that you have known for three years. Before providing the references make sure you read the accompanying guidance notes.

Unlike normal job applications the Local Advisory Committee will make thorough checks with your nominated referees so it is important that you are confident they will support you in your application and provide suitable responses to their questions.

FINAL TIPS FOR COMPLETING A SUCCESSFUL APPLICATION

• Set aside plenty of time to complete your application form. We would recommend at least two evenings work will be sufficient to give it justice – excuse the pun!

• Before you complete the application form make sure you photocopy it if you are intending to complete a written version.

• Read the guidance notes very carefully before completing your form.

• If you are completing the form in your own hand-writing then make sure you use a black pen or other indicated colour.

• It is very important that you learn the role of a magistrate and also the key qualities required in order to perform the role competently. This will enable you to cully understand what the Local Advisory Committee assessors are looking for from potential candidates.

• Try to use keywords and phrases that are relevant to the role when responding to the questions which relate to your reasons for applying.

• If you are completing a written version of the form then make sure your handwriting is clear and easy to read. You should make no punctuation, grammar or spelling errors. Get someone to read your completed form back to you before submitting it. If they struggle to read any part of the form then the assessors will have the same problem too!

• When you have finished completing the form you must make a photocopy of it as you will need it during your preparation for the first and second interviews.

- We recommend that you send off your application form recorded delivery. There have been cases where application forms have become lost in the post. By sending it recorded delivery you will have peace of mind that it has arrived safely.

Now that we have taken the time to look at how to complete a successful application form we will move on to the next stage of the selection process which is the first interview.

CHAPTER 9
THE FIRST INTERVIEW

Although being called for a first interview is a positive and encouraging event it must be remembered that:

- applicants whose paperwork is in order and who are not automatically disqualified will often receive a first interview as a matter of course

- this first interview will last for only around 35-40 minutes, so you will have to be highly focused on what is likely to be covered.

The interview will be held in a public building (often, but not necessarily, a courthouse) and the panel will comprise three (or, exceptionally, two) members, one of whom will usually be a non-magistrate, so the latter may come at matters very differently from the magistrate members. He or she will be an ordinary member of the public just as you are and may ask more general questions of the kind that concern ordinary people, especially in and around the town, city or rural area

where you live or work. You can only really prepare for this by being alive to the key issues and debates that are current in your own community and society in general.

But try to think 'objective opinion' rather than 'overtly political stance'. Justice itself is 'politics' neutral and if you join the bench you will be surprised at how people with sometimes strong and differing political opinions come together to look at matters jointly, in a fair and even-handed way, free of preconceptions. Try to show that you can do this.

If you do need to offer a personal view because not to do so might make you seem a bit indifferent, try adding, in your own words, something to the effect of 'But that's my view and I realise that on the bench I will need to keep it to myself and look at things even-handedly and in a more rounded way'. This kind of reaction ought to be second nature; just as you should be careful never to denigrate or single out people who are 'different'. Everyone must be treated with human dignity and all points of view respected.

Interviews are usually not overly formal and the panel may introduce themselves by their forenames and may even ask if you are happy with that form of address – the aim is to be respectful and dignified but not stuffy.

You do not need 'to buy a new outfit' for the occasions, but do dress and conduct yourself in such a way as to show respect for the process and the role you are seeking to undertake. Because courts are solemn places dealing with things that affect other people's lives, a convention of 'sober dress' is generally observed, but equally this is a modern day and age. The last thing you want to do is look as if you have been kitted out by the 'props department'. You will have already seen magistrates in court during your observation visit(s) and this should have removed any misleading stereotypes that you may have had I mind.

The first interview will concentrate on four main aspects:

- checking, updating and exploring further what was on the original application form

- putting the 'Good Character and Background' question fairly early on

- concentrating on matters such as criminal justice issues and your pre-interview court visits/observations

- the two 'demonstrated/not demonstrated' Key Qualities of 'Commitment and Reliability' and 'Good Character' (please refer to the earlier 'Tips' section for advice on both of these).

However, preliminary views will be formed on all six of the Key Qualities insofar as the opportunity to assess them has arisen - so do keep all six in mind.

Advisory Committees try to give each applicant a broadly similar interview experience. Locally, they will have pre-agreed the sort of questions to be asked and by which member of the panel.

At the first interview you may thus be asked questions along the lines:

- What were your first impressions when you did your court observations?

- What sort of cases did you see?

- What sort of procedures did you see?

- Did anything surprise you?

- What was your view of the decisions the magistrates made and the reasons they gave?

- How would you have approached any of those decisions?

- What impression did your form of the roles of all the other main 'players' in the courtroom? (you will have seen that, centrally, these are the defendant, court legal adviser, Crown prosecutor, defence solicitors, probation officers, police officers, prisoner escorts or possibly prison officers, witnesses and the press)

- What do you think are the main crime problems in your area (or in the country)?

- What factors do you think cause people to commit offences?

- What are your views on the recreational use of drugs?

- What particular factors do you think might give rise to youth crime?

- Have you (or somebody very close to you) ever been the victim of a crime and, if so, what was it and how did you feel about it?

- Did your views change, and if so how, when you learned more about the defendants you saw appearing in court? (remember here that people appearing before the magistrates are innocent unless and until proved guilty: so they only become 'offenders' if and when they are convicted and are about to be sentenced). If the situation arises, try to show that you understand this important difference.

- What is the best way to stop people: (a) offending in the first place and; (b) re-offending when sentenced?

- What is your understanding of the basic and wider commitments of being a magistrate?

- How do you see yourself organising your life to meet those commitments?

- Why do you want to be a magistrate?

- If you want to volunteer a contribution to society, why in this particular way?

- What were the reactions of your family and employer when you said you were applying?

- What would you get personally from being a magistrate?

- What would you bring to the role?

- What do you think the downsides might be of being a magistrate?

- Do you think that the media is always right about crime?

- Do you yourself have any questions of the panel?

Further sample interview questions and how to answer them

Q. Tell us about yourself?

When responding to this question try to focus on the skills and experiences that you have that are relevant to the role of a magistrate. For example:

"Hello, my name is Robert and I'm 38 years old from Leeds. I live in a stable home environment with my partner Debbie of 12 years. We have 3 wonderful children who are all currently at school. I work as a manager for a local large retail centre and I am responsible for the day to day smooth running of the operation. Within my job I have to deal with a diverse range of problems and I also get to meet many people from the local community which I very much enjoy. Because of my job I am a very good listener and I have taken on a voluntary role for a couple of hours during the weekend at the local Citizens Advise Bureau.

In my spare time I enjoy fishing and going on walks with my family. I enjoy keeping fit and I am a member of my local gym. I have also recently successfully completed a distance learning course in management."

Q. Can you tell us why you want to become a magistrate?

You will have already answered this question during the application form stage. Make sure you read your response on the application form prior to attending the interview, as the response you use should not be too dissimilar.

Q. What has attracted you to the role?

Only you will know what has attracted you to the role. The following list will assist you in your preparation for this type of question.

What to say

- Making a difference to the community;

- Interacting with people from the community;

- The challenge that the role will bring;

- The commitment and responsibility;

- The opportunity to use existing skills and develop new ones;

- The variety of the role. No two days will be the same;

What not say

- Punishing criminals;

- Locking people away who deserve it;

- That people in society will respect you.

Q. What do you think the qualities are that a magistrate needs to have in order to perform the role competently?

During your initial research into the role you will have learnt a tremendous amount. You will need to explain this during your response to this type of question. The following are examples of the types of qualities required to perform the role:

- An ability to communicate effectively both verbally and in writing;

- Being able to remain calm, focused and non confrontational;

- A level of assertiveness when required;

- Professionalism and pride;

- Reliable and committed;

- Motivated and a willingness to learn;

- A good character;

- Be able to understand situations;

- Be aware of society;

- Have a sound temperament.

The above list is not exhaustive and you may have noticed more relevant qualities when visiting your local magistrate's court.

Q. Do you have the support of your employer? What do they think about your application?

As you are aware you will need to have the full support of your employer before you apply. Make sure you discuss your intentions with your employer before you attend the interview.

Q. What do you think the job of a magistrate involves?

In order to answer this question effectively you will need to read this guide thoroughly and also read your recruitment literature. Within the literature you will be provided with plenty of information that relates to the role. It is also a good idea to inform the interview panel what you learnt about the role during your visit to your local magistrates' court. The definitive role of a magistrate however is as follows:

As a magistrate, you will sit in your local magistrates' court dealing with a wide range of less serious criminal cases and civil matters. Some of your duties will include:

- determining whether a defendant is guilty or not and passing the appropriate sentence;

- deciding on requests for remand in custody;

- deciding on applications for bail;

- committing more serious cases to the Crown Court.

With experience and further training you could also go on to deal with cases in the family and youth courts. Magistrates sit on a 'bench' of three (an experienced chairman with two other magistrates) and are accompanied in court by a trained legal advisor to give guidance on the law and sentencing options. (Source: Crown Copyright ©)

Q. What skills or experiences can you bring to the magistracy?

The response you provide to this question will very much depend on the experiences you already have to date. Try to think about the role and the qualities required to become a magistrate and match them with your own life experiences and skills.

Q. What interests and activities do you have outside of the work environment?

Once again you will already have provided a response to this type of question when completing the application form. Be prepared for further probing questions in this area, especially for outside activities that relate to community of voluntary work.

Q. Have you ever carried out any form of community or voluntary work either locally or nationally?

It would be an advantage if you can provide some evidence of community or voluntary work during the interview. Candidates who can provide evidence of this are more likely to score higher than those who do not. If you have evidence of any community work then it would be worthwhile taking this along with your to the interview. Be prepared for additional questions in this area such as *"What did you learn from the experience"* and *"Didn't you find it frustrating not getting paid?"*

Q. Tell us about the community in which you live in? What do you know about it?

If you have already experience a level of community or voluntary work then this question will be easier for you to respond to. As a magistrate you will need to have an understanding of your community and the local issues affecting it. A sample response to this question would be:

"Having lived in this area for a few years now, and having carried out local community work, I am fully aware of the community and more importantly its needs. As with all communities ours is extremely diverse in nature which is a great thing. Diversity brings many positive aspects to society as I have witnessed during my time. I am also aware that

there a number of problems in this community in relation to burglary, especially from domestic houses. I understand that the local Police Force are doing everything they can to solve the problems and whilst I was visiting my local magistrates court I witnessed a trial which involved such a case. Obviously every case must be judged on its own merits which I believe I have the skills to do. It is important that everyone within the community, both here and nationally, is treated fairly, and with dignity and respect."

Q. What experience do you have of working with people from different backgrounds or cultures to yourself?

As a magistrate you will be required to work with, and interact with, people from many different backgrounds and cultures without any prejudice. If you can provide examples of where you have worked with people from different backgrounds and cultures then this will work in your favour.

Q. On your application form you have stated that you have visited your local magistrates' court. Tell us about that experience and what you learnt from it?

When you visit your local magistrates' court it is advisable that you take along with you a pencil and a notebook. This will enable you to take down key notes and information that you learn from your experience. When you are asked questions about your visit to the court then you will be able to provide clear evidence of what you have learnt.

Q. How do you feel about the role being voluntary and therefore not getting paid, apart from expenses?

As you will be fully aware the role of a magistrate is voluntary. Whilst you will be able to claim for certain expenses you will need to be comfortable with the fact that it is not a paid role. A sample response to this type of question might be:

"I am fully comfortable with this. The benefit to me would be in the fact that I would be giving something back to the community and also that I would be learning a tremendous amount from the experience. The monetary rewards for such a role are irrelevant."

Q. How do you go about making decisions in life? What's your thought process?

As a magistrate you will have a huge responsibility for making important decisions about key facts and events. The ability to make sound judgements is therefore crucial. How you make decisions in your work and personal life may have an impact on how you make decisions as a magistrate. Here is a sample response to this type of question:

"Before I make any decision in life I always make sure that I gather the full facts and I am never influenced by stereotypes or prejudice. I understand that as a magistrate there is a huge responsibility to listen carefully to the facts of the case and treat each one on its own merits. It is important not to jump to conclusions but instead to listen to the facts carefully before making informed decisions."

Q. What are the advantages for you in becoming a magistrate?

Only you will know the true advantages to yourself in becoming a magistrate. However, here is a sample response to assist you in your preparation:

"I believe there would be many advantages for becoming a magistrate. The first and most important would be working in a worthwhile role that has a benefit to the community. This is a highly responsible role and roles of this nature are things that I really enjoy.

The other advantage would be the ability to influence and make a positive impact to the community. I also very much enjoy working with people from different ages, backgrounds, genders and cultures and I believe this role would allow me to do just that."

Q. Do you think there could be any disadvantages for you in becoming a magistrate?

Before you apply to become a magistrate you will have no doubt explored the role in depth and decide whether the role is of benefit to you or not. If there are any disadvantages then you may want to think twice before applying.

Q. What does your family think about you wanting to become a magistrate?

Before you apply to become a magistrate you should discuss carefully your choice of role and in particular how it might impact on your family. Remember that you will be required to commit to at least 26 sittings per year and there will also be the additional training commitment(s). When responding to questions of this nature try to explain that your family are fully supportive of your decision and that you have already planned for the commitments just in case you are successful.

Q. What do your friends think about you wanting to become a magistrate?

Before responding to questions of this nature it is advisable that you think carefully about what you believe the interview panel want to hear. Take a look at the following two sample responses and it should become clear which one is the more appropriate:

Sample response 1
"Having discussed it with all of my friends they are just as

excited as I am about the possibility of me becoming a magistrate. Already people are starting to treat me differently and give me a higher level of respect!"

Sample response 2

"I haven't discussed my application with any of my friends as I believe it to be a confidential role. I am a discreet person and wouldn't feel comfortable with promoting my application amongst my peers. However, if they were to find out that I was applying to become a magistrate then I am sure they would wish me well."

Sample 2 is obviously a more appropriate response. Remember that two of the key qualities of a magistrate are maturity and confidentiality.

Q. Can you provide an example of where you have had to consult other people before making a difficult decision?

As you are aware, part of the magistrate's role is to discuss and consult other magistrates before making decisions about specific cases. The Local Advisory Committee will not recommend applicants who are either controlling or dictatorial. Whilst you may have plenty of life experiences you must be capable of listening to other people's views and also consulting with those people before making important life changing decisions.

Q. If you are to be successful in your application, what training would you undergo?

Within your application pack you will have received details on the type of training you will undergo if you are to be successful in your application. Make sure you read it and learn it as this will demonstrate a level of commitment and motivation.

INTERVIEW TECHNIQUE

How you present yourself during the interview is important. Take a look at the following diagrams, which indicate both poor technique and good technique.

POOR INTERVIEW TECHNIQUE

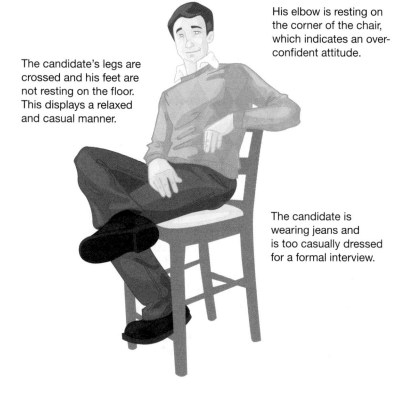

His elbow is resting on the corner of the chair, which indicates an over-confident attitude.

The candidate's legs are crossed and his feet are not resting on the floor. This displays a relaxed and casual manner.

The candidate is wearing jeans and is too casually dressed for a formal interview.

The candidate appears to be too relaxed and casual for an interview.

GOOD INTERVIEW TECHNIQUE

The candidate is smiling and he portrays a confident, but not over-confident manner.

The candidate is dressed wearing a smart suit. It is clear that he has made an effort in his presentation.

His hands are in a stable position, which will prevent him from fidgeting. He could also place his hands palms facing downwards and resting on his knees.

He is sitting upright in the interview chair with his feet resting on the floor. He is not slouching and he portrays himself in a positive manner.

IMPROVING INTERVIEW TECHNIQUE

- When you walk into the interview room make sure you smile and be courteous towards the panel. It is good practice to shake their hand if you feel comfortable to do so.

- Do not sit down in the interview chair until invited to do so. This displays good manners and common courtesy.

- Throughout the interview be respectful towards the panel.

- When you are sat in the interview chair sit up right and do not slouch.

- You must wear a formal outfit to the interview. This is important as you are applying for a highly responsible position. Avoid bright coloured clothes, socks or ties! Try to think about the general 'conservative' atmosphere in court and dress in an appropriate manner during your interview.

- Try to communicate in a clear and concise manner throughout the interview. One of the key qualities of a magistrate is having the ability to communicate effectively both verbally and in writing.

- During the interview speak with confidence but never become overbearing or arrogant.

- If you are unsure of the response to an interview question then it is ok to say so. Never try to waffle and do not lie as you will get caught out either at the interview, or at some point in the future.

- At the end of the interview it is acceptable to ask one or two questions. However, the questions you decide to ask

should be mature and relevant to the role. Examples of good questions to ask are:

Q. If I am to be successful how long would it be before I commenced my training?

Q. Would there be the opportunity in the distant future to become a mentor, providing I meet the grade and gain sufficient experience?

Once you have successfully passed the first interview you will then be invited to attend a second, more formal interview. We will now move onto the next section of the guide which will provide you with tips and advice on how to prepare for this final stage

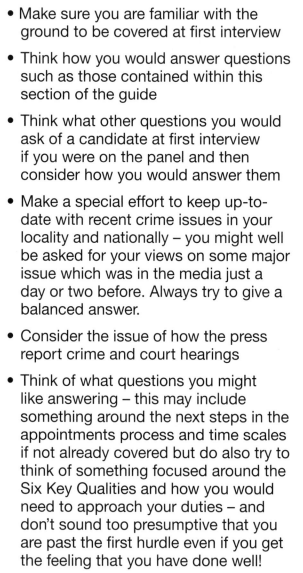

SOME THINGS TO DO

- Make sure you are familiar with the ground to be covered at first interview

- Think how you would answer questions such as those contained within this section of the guide

- Think what other questions you would ask of a candidate at first interview if you were on the panel and then consider how you would answer them

- Make a special effort to keep up-to-date with recent crime issues in your locality and nationally – you might well be asked for your views on some major issue which was in the media just a day or two before. Always try to give a balanced answer.

- Consider the issue of how the press report crime and court hearings

- Think of what questions you might like answering – this may include something around the next steps in the appointments process and time scales if not already covered but do also try to think of something focused around the Six Key Qualities and how you would need to approach your duties – and don't sound too presumptive that you are past the first hurdle even if you get the feeling that you have done well!

CHAPTER 10
THE SECOND INTERVIEW

If you have performed well enough at first interview (i.e. to at least the extent that the panel does not recommend against a second interview) you will be offered a second one, usually five to 15 working days later so the timescale may be tight.

The second interview will involve:

- discussing two previously unseen case study exercises that will be handed to you on arrival for the interview – around 30 minutes only will be allowed for you to think about how you will answer both - a ranking exercise and an individual case study (both as described further below) before going into the interview

- an interview lasting about 40-50 minutes.

The interview panel will again usually comprise three members (with at least one being a non-magistrate). Membership may differ from the first panel, although there is sometimes one member from the first interview which will serve to ensure some carry over.

The above may sound a bit daunting but, again, remember that the panel is trying to see the 'real you' so, if you know what to expect, you should be able to give a good account of yourself.

THE FIRST CASE EXERCISE: RANKING THE SERIOUSNESS OF OFFENCES

The first exercise will give you around ten micro-scenarios and you will be asked to rank them in order of seriousness as you see matters. There is no need to 'panic' as there is no 'right or wrong' answer, although:

- you will be asked to explain what you took into account in each scenario and why you ranked them in the way you did.

- you may be asked to comment on an opposing view of the ranking order.

- you need to show that you are prepared to listen to, and consider fairly, any contrary views the panel may put to you (don't feel devalued or overly defensive in your ranking as they may be taking a contrary view solely for the sake of the exercise. Whatever, be positive, but make clear that you understand differences of opinion, are open-minded and fully considering any counter-views, that you are not being 'precious' about your own view.

- you will need to reflect that there may be legal or guideline aggravating or mitigating factors (see e.g. the 2008 Magistrates' Court Sentencing Guidelines at www. sentencing-guidelines.gov.uk) that you must or must not take into account (you will later be trained in the use of these if you are appointed and need not learn them now).

- you should specifically consider the harm done or likely to be done by an offence and the level of the offender's culpability.

The scenarios might include, for example:

- assault on a police constable

- possession of drugs

- possession of indecent pictures of children

- domestic violence (by either partner)

- theft

- burglary.

More substantial examples appear in the 'Sample Ranking Exercise' provided within this section of your guide. In their way all will probably be serious and the basis of the exercise is to see what factors you think make up that seriousness and whether you can weigh say the effect of the theft of a purse from a pensioner by going into his or her house through an open door against the impact of domestic violence on a young child who might witness it going on between his or her parents.

If you understand the nature and process of this exercise in advance you should have no difficulty in arriving at a measured response in readiness for discussion in the short time available. It is the way in which you arrive at your answer that will be important, not whether you have placed everything in some 'correct' order.

Expect to answer questions such as:

Q. Why do did you place [a particular choice] at the top of your list?

Q. What if the burglary was at night and the intruder had a weapon?

Q. Why did you place [a particular choice] after [another choice]?

SAMPLE RANKING EXERCISE

All interview panels set up by Advisory Committees will, at the second interview, use a form of Ranking Exercise approved by the Ministry of Justice. The actual format and content may vary but the basic task will be broadly the same:

1. From a list of ten or so briefly described offences you will be asked to pick say the four that you consider to be the most serious.

2. You will then be asked what factors in those four made you consider them to be the most serious – remember there will be no 'right or wrong' answer.

3. You may also be asked which you think was the most serious of the four you chose and why.

4. You may also be asked what factors you identified in the other six offences.

Important tips to consider

1. The facts will be straightforwardly and briefly stated for you – there should not be too much detail to get to grips with.

2. This exercise requires no prior knowledge of court work or sentencing – it is your own, immediate impressions that will be sought.

3. Although some offences may at the extremes be less serious than others it might help to indentify and note briefly

(using your own 'nudge' words) the salient features of each offence and then pick your four most serious:

a) this way, and given the limited time available, you won't pick your four by gut reaction and then feel the need to spend precious time revising once you start listing the seriousness factors.

b) magistrates are trained to analyse cases and facts before they reach any decision – this focuses the decision-making process and also helps with the reasons for the final decision.

4. Look for factors in the way offences were committed which make them more or less serious of their type and in relation to different types of offences.

5. Consider also any factors about the offender you may be given.

Here is a sample Ranking Exercise for you to try. Write down your thoughts/observations in the 'relevant features' box and prioritise the 4 most serious (in your opinion) on the right hand side.

FACTS	RELEVANT FEATURES	FOUR MOST SERIOUS
Ambulance called to a young woman who has collapsed outside a nightclub. The girl's female companion is drunk, insults and shoves the crew, kicks in the headlight of their ambulance and is then arrested by passing police.		

FACTS	RELEVANT FEATURES	FOUR MOST SERIOUS
A 35 year-old woman is stopped for drink-driving (just over the limit) on her way to collect her husband two miles away who missed the last bus home from work. It transpires that she is just about to finish a six-month driving ban for 'totting up' because she earlier reached 12 points.		
A 40-year-old man has recently been released from prison having served three months for a sex offence on a child. Being a registered sex offender he told the police that he would be living with his mother on release. Instead he has gone to live with his girlfriend and her two young children		
An 18 year-old sixth-former has been found to have 30 ecstasy tablets in his school bag. He claims that they were for personal use and he did not want his parents to find them at home.		

FACTS	RELEVANT FEATURES	FOUR MOST SERIOUS
A 50 year-old man is passing an elderly widow's sheltered housing bungalow and sees the glass front door open and her handbag on the hall table. He sneaks in and steals the handbag which contains that week's pension money.		
Members at a local family tennis club smell cannabis and trace it to a 40 year-old coach who kept a small amount in his locker and smoked it between giving lessons to youngsters.		
On a wet afternoon, a 55 year-old man, late for a business meeting, drives his new 4x4 at 42 mph in a 30 mph area near a school as the pupils are just leaving		
A 30 year-old man has a row with his wife at home and pushes her against a cupboard causing her some bruising about the head and face.		

FACTS	RELEVANT FEATURES	FOUR MOST SERIOUS
A 25 year-old woman who is a local heroin user walks out of her local supermarket with a DVD recorder under her arm and, when challenged by the security guard, knees him in the groin and tries to flee.		
A 30 year-old woman has a row with her husband in a pub and pushes him over a bar table causing him lacerations to his arm and back from broken glasses.		

Once you have completed the table and chosen your 4 most serious offences, take the time to read the following table which has the relevant features boxes completed by a magistrate.

FACTS	RELEVANT FEATURES	FOUR MOST SERIOUS
Ambulance called to a young woman who has collapsed outside a nightclub. The girl's female companion is drunk, insults and shoves the crew, kicks in the headlight of their ambulance and is then arrested by passing police.	- Drunkenness is no excuse - Offence against public servant - Ambulance probably out of use for some time - possible effect on others who need emergency services - General public nuisance	**?**
A 35 year-old woman is stopped for drink-driving (just over the limit) on her way to collect her husband two miles away who missed the last bus home from work. It transpires that she is just about to finish a six-month driving ban for 'totting up' because she earlier reached 12 points.	- Nature of offence even if just over the limit - Breach of earlier court order - Short distance (but many accidents occur near to home?)	**?**

FACTS	RELEVANT FEATURES	FOUR MOST SERIOUS
A 40-year-old man has recently been released from prison having served three months for a sex offence on a child. Being a registered sex offender he told the police that he would be living with his mother on release. Instead he has gone to live with his girlfriend and her two young children	- In breach of the sex offender register provisions either by not telling truth on release or changing mind and then not notifying	?
An 18 year-old sixth-former has been found to have 30 ecstasy tablets in his school bag. He claims that they were for personal use and he did not want his parents to find them at home.	- Drugs in a school environment - Possible effect on younger pupils - Not charged as 'possession with intent to supply' but a lot of tablets for own use	?
A 50 year-old man is passing an elderly widow's sheltered housing bungalow and sees the glass front door open and her handbag on the hall table. He sneaks in and steals the handbag which contains that week's pension money.	- Opportunist and not forcible entry - Must have known victim likely to be elderly and possibly of limited means? - General effect of burglary on victims	?

FACTS	RELEVANT FEATURES	FOUR MOST SERIOUS
Members at a local family tennis club smell cannabis and trace it to a 40 year-old coach who kept a small amount in his locker and smoked it between giving lessons to youngsters.	- Small amount and for personal use - Views on cannabis have varied - Effect on other members - Possibly children about	?
On a wet afternoon, a 55 year-old man, late for a business meeting, drives his new 4x4 at 42 mph in a 30 mph area near a school as the pupils are just leaving	- Not the highest of excess speeds - Brakes, steering etc may be in excellent condition - But extra danger near school - Driver may have been concentrating on his lateness	?
A 30 year-old man has a row with his wife at home and pushes her against a cupboard causing her some bruising about the head and face.	- 'Domestic violence' in a private setting? - Male assaulting a female - A push or was it worse? - Injuries not the most serious?	?

FACTS	RELEVANT FEATURES	FOUR MOST SERIOUS
A 25 year-old woman who is a local heroin user walks out of her local supermarket with a DVD recorder under her arm and, when challenged by the security guard, knees him in the groin and tries to flee.	- Nature of assault - Likely to have been children and families present	**?**
A 30 year-old woman has a row with her husband in a pub and pushes him over a bar table causing him lacerations to his arm and back from broken glasses.	- Female assaulting a male - 'Domestic violence' in a public setting - A push or was it worse? - Injuries quite serious	**?**

THE SECOND CASE EXERCISE: A MORE DETAILED INDIVIDUAL CASE STUDY

The second exercise will be a single, fuller case scenario, more than likely based on sentencing practice. You will not be required to have any knowledge of sentencing aims, practices or actual disposals and there will, again, be no real 'right or wrong' answer. It might, however, be worth being aware that there are the following four broad ascending levels of sentencing, each of which has its own sort of 'threshold' test:

- absolute or conditional discharge (i.e. re the latter, broadly no penalty unless there is reoffending)

- fine (based on both the seriousness of the offence and the offender's financial circumstances and up to £5,000 in more serious cases in the magistrates' court)

- community order (e.g. supervision by a probation officer, curfew order, undertaking a rehabilitative programme: this is now a generic order within which there can be various components of this kind)

- imprisonment (aka 'custody') (which can be suspended if appropriate).

Sometimes more than one sentence can be used at the same time but you will not be expected to know the ins-and-outs of this. The exercise will again test how you approach the problem. What is important here are matters such as:

- how you deal with the overall decision-making process

- what issues you identify as relevant

- what you might be trying to achieve in sentencing

- whether and how you think a pre-sentence report ('PSR') from the National Probation Service might assist in sentencing (what would you expect it to tell you that you have not already heard from the Crown prosecutor and the defence solicitor)

- where you would broadly pitch your sentencing

- how you react to having to consider giving up to one third 'credit' or 'discount' against sentence for a (timely) guilty plea

- whether you are able and willing to refer to guidance and to seek/take advice.

Again, you must be ready to explain your views and to listen

attentively and respond to opposing views in a balanced way. An example of a case study appears at the end of this section. The 'Good Character and Background' question will be put again, this time probably at the end of the interview. You will again also be invited to ask questions.

It is at the end of the second interview that the panel will complete its formal assessment 'scores' and recommendations to the full Advisory Committee.

SOME THINGS TO DO

- Make sure you are familiar with the ground to be covered at the second interview

- Think how you would answer questions on the above matters

- Think what other questions you would ask of a candidate at second interview if you were on the panel and then consider how you would answer them

- Make a special effort to keep up-to-date with recent crime issues in your locality and nationally – you might well be asked your views on some major issue such as the early release of prisoners, knife crime, or anti-social behaviour which was in the media just a day or two ago

- Think how you might objectively approach a case of the kind you may have heard of or seen reported recently

- Think of what questions you might like answering – again this may often include something around the next steps in the appointments process and time scales if not already covered but do also try to think of something more aimed at the Six Key Qualities and how you would need to approach your duties. Again, don't presume that you are through but be confident having prepared well in accordance with this guide.

SAMPLE CASE STUDY

Consider the following facts:

- Robbo is aged 18.

- He lives at home with his divorced mother who is supporting him financially during his full-time IT course at the local college.

- He has just pleaded guilty at the first hearing to three offences of racially aggravated criminal damage.

- Late one Sunday evening he had super-glued A3 size posters (which he had run off on the college's photocopier) on the windows of each of three shops in the local precinct, the Star of India Restaurant, Patel's Newsagents and Chinatown Takeaway.

- The posters said 'Go back where you belong' and included racist images.

- It took a specialist cleaning firm most of Monday morning to remove the posters and clean the windows.

- He has no previous convictions.

- His course is due to finish in three months time and he has just joined an agency to look for temporary office work for when he finishes.

How might you answer the following sample questions at interview (and what reasons would you give):

1. At what level (say fine, community-based order or custody) would you normally pitch criminal damage by defacement which leaves no permanent damage (e.g. graffiti or fly-posting)?

2. What makes the present offences more or less serious than other offences of criminal damage by defacement?

3. Apart from the obvious inconvenience and cost, what sort of harm might have resulted from Robbo's offences?

4. What personal factors about Robbo do you think might affect how you would want to sentence him?

5. How would you feel if you were advised that you might be able base any financial penalty against Robbo on the fact that his mother is maintaining him at present?

6. Allowing for the fact that you are not expected to have any technical knowledge about sentencing, what, in broad terms, would you like your sentence to look like?

7. Assuming that Robbo's funds are limited; would you prefer to give priority to a fine, compensating the business owners or meeting the public costs of bringing the prosecution?

8. How would you feel if advised that, because he has pleaded guilty at the first opportunity, you should reduce Robbo's sentence by around one third.

9. How, if at all, would your approach differ if Robbo had previously been subject to an Ant-Social Behaviour Order (ASBO) for painting graffiti which expired 18 months ago?

In the half-hour you will have on the day to consider the Case Study along with the Ranking Exercise you might find it appropriate again to make a few notes to 'nudge' you and on which to build in the interview. Try this with the sample exercise and try and stick to 30 minutes to 'get you in training'. Compare what you noted down with how somebody else might have approached the case as described below:

1. Usually a fine but community order (perhaps unpaid work) might be appropriate if e.g.

- a) More serious in nature
- b) Previous convictions.

2. Aggravated by e.g.

- a) Racial element
- b) Number of offences
- c) Obviously pre-planned.

3. Other harm would include:

- a) Victims would feel racially offended
- b) Victims might fear personal attacks
- c) Effect on local community relations
- d) Other members of ethnic minorities might feel offended or in fear
- e) Possible loss of business.

4. Personal factors might include:

- a) Comparative youth
- b) Lack of means
- c) May 'grow out of it' once he has a job?

5. Finances:

- a) Obviously totally dependent on mother at moment and for immediate future
- b) Should not escape a financial penalty (if appropriate) just because he draws his means from someone else
- c) Equally mother should not be unduly penalised
- d) He may have a job in the near future
- e) Could look for some part-time work now.

6. Broad sentence:

   a) Community order perhaps with unpaid work and/or programme to address racial views

   b) Compensation to extent possible and permitted by guidelines

   c) Might look at custody if repeated.

7. Priority:

   a) Compensation

   b) Fine

   c) Costs.

8. Reduction by a third:

   a) Has saved time and the need for the victims to undergo the experience of giving evidence in court

   b) Would reduce if so required – reduction preferable to unpaid work but not a programme to address offending behaviour.

9. ASBO:

   a) Not in breach

   b) But shows predisposition

   c) May strengthen the need for more than a fine (what are the further facts?).

WHAT HAPPENS NEXT?

This guide is not intended as an account of what will happen if you are successful in your application, but it may help you to understand the process better to know that in due course:

- you will receive a letter of appointment

- you will need to be sworn in (usually at a ceremony with other new magistrates who will become your colleagues in training)

- you will undertake initial training within the scheme provided for by the Magistrates National Training Initiative (universally known as MINTI, or MINTI 2 as it is now in its second phase of development)

- you will undertake your first court sittings under the watchful but helpful eye of senior colleagues and staff who will be dedicated to making sure that you 'learn the ropes' and succeed in your new role.

'AT A GLANCE' TIMESCALE GUIDE CONCERNING YOUR APPLICATION

All timescales are illustrative only and may vary according to areas and circumstances

Applications may be submitted at any time
to be held against the annual recruitment cycle

∨

Usually acknowledged within 5 working days of receipt.

∨

Annual publicity and recruitment cycle
(times vary across the country)

∨

Consideration of all pending and new applications.

Any applicants automatically ineligible for appointment usually notified within 10 working daysof receipt of their application.

Any applicants subject to potential ineligibility to be brought to attention of Advisory Committee and the applicant informed within 20 working days of receipt of application if not to be considered.

Other candidates called for first interviews as soon as possible after closing date for annual cycle

This may be over a number of weeks if there are many applicants.

Any second interviews will usually take place 5-15 working days after the relevant first interview.

(Enhanced) CRB checks and Undertakings for those to be recommended for appointment. Timing depends on when all second interviews are complete and committee has considered all reports.

The Lord Chancellor, in liaison with the Lord Chief Justice, considers recommendations of Advisory Committees and appoints as appropriate.

Letter of Appointment

Assignment of mentor, start of initial training (including visits and observations) and swearing-in

Start to sit as a 'winger' in the adult court

12-18 months onwards
Eligible to apply to sit on youth or family work, subject to appraisal (possibly also on appeals at the Crown Court, subject to local arrangements)

Year 5-6 onwards
Eligible to apply to train to take the chair, again subject to appraisal

CHAPTER II
SOME USEFUL WEBSITES
AND CONTACT POINTS

The following have either been identified in the text or are now also worthy of mention.

www.direct.gov.uk
General information about public services including the courts

www.hmcourts-service.gov.uk
How magistrates' courts (and other courts of law) are managed

www.sentencing-guidelines.gov.uk
Guidance and advice to all magistrates and judges, including the Magistrates' Court Sentencing Guidelines

www.magistrates-association.org.uk
The key membership organization which you may wish to join once appointed as a magistrate (the vast majority

of magistrates do join 'the MA') and which also has a considerable amount of information freely available at it's website. You will see that the application form asks at the end whether, if you are appointed as a magistrate, you would mind your details being given to the association.

www.jc-society.co.uk
The site for legal advisers where you can obtain an idea of their role and professional interests

www.moj.gov.uk
HM Courts Service comes under the Ministry of Justice (MOJ) and the Lord Chancellor and Secretary of State for Justice (to use the full title)(aka 'Justice Secretary') has many responsibilities in relation to (independent) judges and magistrates

You can also contact the following MOJ unit:

The Magistrates' Appointment Team
Ministry of Justice
Magistrates Recruitment and Appointments Branch
Judicial Services Directorate
Room 5.40
5th Floor
102 Petty France
London SW1H 7AJ

E mail: mnrsteam@justice.gsi.gov.uk

www.businesslink.gov.uk
For information about time off work, etc.

For a more detailed guide to the role that you are thinking of taking up, see 'The Magistrates' Court: An Introduction' by Bryan Gibson (Consultant Mike Watkins), Waterside Press (5th. Edn. 2009) (available from www.how2become.co.uk).

Visit www.how2become.co.uk to find more titles and courses that will help you to pass the Magistrate selection process, including:

- 1-Day Magistrate training course

- How to complete the Magistrate Application Form DVD

- How to pass the Magistrate interview

- Psychometric testing books and CDs.

www.how2become.co.uk